Food on the Farm

Written by Catherine Casey

Illustrated by Lee Teng

Collins

The farmer has seeds.

The soil gets wet with rain.

Herbs are in the pots.

The farmer chops herbs.

Leeks are in soil.

The farmer pulls up leeks.

The beetroots are dark pink.

The farmer digs up beetroots.

The corn is high.

The farmer needs to pick it.

The farmer chops the food.

The farmer cooks food.

Seeds to food

After reading

Letters and Sounds: Phase 3

Word count: 60

Focus phonemes: /ai/ /ee/ / igh/ /oo/ /oo/ /ar/ /or/ /oi/ /er/

Common exception words: to, the, pulls, are

Curriculum links: Understanding of the World

Early learning goals: Reading: use phonic knowledge to decode regular words and read them aloud accurately; read and understand simple sentences

Developing fluency

- Ask your child to read their favourite pages as if they were the narrator for a video for schools.
- Encourage them to practise reading all the words clearly. Demonstrate sounding out and blending to check you are reading a word correctly.

Phonic practice

- Challenge your child to find words in the book with the /oo/ and /oo/ phonemes:
  - oo as in zoo (*food*, *beetroots*)
  - *oo* as in look (*cooks*)
- Ask your child to find words that contain the /er/ phoneme (*herbs*, *farmer*).

Extending vocabulary

- Look at the verbs on pages 5, 7 and 13. Ask your child to think of similar words (synonyms) that could be used in their place:
  - **chops** (e.g. *cuts*, *dices*, *minces*)
  - **pulls** (e.g. *tugs*, *yanks*, *hauls*)
  - **cooks** (e.g. *bakes*, *boils*, *steams*)